P9-CEQ-446

I WAS A
THIRD GRADE
SCIENCE PROJECT

YEARLING BOOKS are designed especially to entertain and enlighten young people. Patricia Reilly Giff, consultant to this series, received her bachelor's degree from Marymount College and a master's degree in history from St. John's University. She holds a Professional Diploma in Reading and a Doctorate of Humane Letters from Hofstra University. She was a teacher and reading consultant for many years, and is the author of numerous books for young readers.

I WAS A
THIRD GRADE
SCIENCE PROJECT

MARY JANE AUCH

illustrated by Herm Auch

A Yearling Book

Published by
Bantam Doubleday Dell Books for Young Readers
a division of
Random House, Inc.
1540 Broadway
New York, New York 10036

Visit us on the Web! www.randomhouse.com

Educators and librarians, for a variety of teaching tools, visit us at www.randomhouse.com/teachers

ISBN: 0-440-41606-X

Reprinted by arrangement with Holiday House

Printed in the United States of America

November 1999

10 9 8 7 6 5 4 3 2 1

OPM

To H. W. A.

M. J. A.

To M. J. A.

H. W. A.

I WAS A
THIRD GRADE
SCIENCE PROJECT

CHAPTER ONE

Having a genius for a friend can be real trouble. I know, because my best friend is Brian Lewis. All the other kids in third grade call him Brain. I don't, because he doesn't like it. He calls me Josh, even though some kids call me Birdbrain. It's not that I'm stupid, but when you hang around with a genius, you don't look like the smartest person in the world.

I could see trouble coming when Mrs. Metz made the big announcement. "Boys and girls, now that you're third graders, you'll get to enter a project in the Ontario Elementary Science Fair. I know you've all been looking forward to it."

There was a moan in the back of the room from Dougie Hanks, who thought the only thing to look forward to in school was the last bell.

Mrs. Metz shot him a look and kept going. "I'm going to let you pick your own partners. You need to plan an experiment and work with it at home for the next three weeks. You'll keep journals of your observations, and they will be judged for originality."

Emily Venable waved her hand frantically. "Will this count toward our grade, Mrs. Metz?"

"Yes, Emily, it will be part of your science grade, but there's even more at stake here. The three winning teams from each classroom will present their projects on Parents' Night. A grand prize team will be picked from each grade level and they'll get free passes for their families to use at Wonderland Lake this summer."

Even I was interested in this. Wonderland Lake just happened to be the best amusement park in the whole state. We hardly ever got to go, because Dad said it was too expensive.

Emily's hand was waving again. "Who are the judges, Mrs. Metz?"

"This class will be judged by the other third grade teachers and the principal. None of us will be judging our own classes until Parents' Night, when all of the judges will vote on the grand prize winners."

Emily slumped back into her chair. Being teacher's pet wasn't going to get her any points this time.

Mrs. Metz passed out instruction sheets and went on to explain what an experiment was. I heard her say things like "observation" and "recording results," but I wasn't paying much attention. I was remembering my first and only ride on Screaming Mimi, Wonderland's roller coaster. I threw up three times. It was the best ride I've ever been on.

I didn't bother to listen to the instructions, because Brian would find out what we needed to know. Sure enough, his head was bobbing up and down like a yo-yo by the time Mrs. Metz finished.

"You can take the time between now and the end of school to find a partner and talk about what you want to do," Mrs. Metz said. "I'll have a sign-up list ready on Monday."

Brian's desk was right next to mine. He leaned across the aisle. "We'll be partners, right? Got any ideas?"

I tried to remember what I'd seen when our second grade teacher had taken us through last year's Science Fair exhibit. "We could do one of those papier-mâché volcanoes with green goop oozing out of it," I said.

Brian frowned. "Lava is red when it's hot. Besides, you heard what Mrs. Metz said. We're being judged on originality. The volcano has been done a million times. We need something we can watch every day and take notes on." Brian was very big on taking notes in *cursive*. He scribbled in his notebook. "We need to observe something growing or changing."

"Okay, I've got it," I said. "How about we

plant seeds in two pots? Then we'll water one and not the other and see which one grows best."

"That's no fun," Brian said. "We know which one will grow best."

"Mrs. Metz never said it had to be fun," I said. I was planning to be the one to *not* water the plants.

Brian got a faraway look in his eyes. "We have to think of something nobody's ever done before," he said.

I could sense trouble coming. "If you're dreaming up another flying garbage can project and you want me to be the test pilot, you can forget it. My flying and crashing days are over."

The final bell snapped Brian out of his trance. "Never mind," he said. "We'll come up with a great project when you sleep over tonight."

I arrived at Brian's house right after dinner. The Lewises were still eating when I got there.

"Have a seat, Josh," Mrs. Lewis said. "Would you like some quinoa pilaf?" She held out a bowl of tiny round things that had little white worms wrapped around them.

"No thanks, Mrs. Lewis. I ate already." I would have said that even if I was starving.

"Quinoa is very high in protein, Josh. This is the very grain eaten by the ancient Incas. It was one of their staples, along with corn and potatoes. Did you know that?"

I didn't, but if the stuff had been around that long, that would explain the worms.

Brian must have read my mind. "The white things aren't worms, Josh. It's just the germ of the grain."

Germs? This was supposed to make me feel better? Poor Brian never got a normal meal.

As soon as he was excused, Brian dragged me up to his room. His dog, Arful, followed us. Arful is a mixture of dog breeds, all of them huge and hairy. He was saved from the dog pound by Brian's mother.

When Arful stood on his hind legs, he could put his paws on my shoulders and lick my face. Now he was licking the fried chicken grease from my dinner. He seemed pretty excited about it. Probably never tasted fried chicken before. Mrs. Lewis never fried anything.

Brian picked up his notebook and a pencil. "Did you come up with an idea yet?"

I shrugged. "No. Not unless you want to do the plant thing."

Brian rolled his eyes. I hate it when he does that. I don't mind him being a genius, but he doesn't have to act like I'm stupid.

"Okay," he said. "How about we measure your height, then have you eat my mother's healthy food every meal for the next three weeks? Then we'll measure you again to see how much you've grown."

"How about we have *you* eat your mother's healthy food and measure you?"

Brian rolled his eyes again, which made me want to smack him. "That's not going to prove anything. I'm already eating healthy. We need someone who eats junk all the time, like you."

"How about you eat junk and we see if you shrink?" I said.

Brian put down his pencil. "I'll think of something later. Let's go watch TV."

Brian gets to watch more TV than any kid I know. His father is a psychiatrist, who has this theory that Brian is so smart, he'll figure out which things are good for him and which things aren't. So, if Brian isn't sleepy, he can stay downstairs and watch TV until three in the morning and nobody yells at him.

That night, Dr. and Mrs. Lewis watched TV with us until they got tired. Mrs. Lewis went out to the kitchen and came back with two glasses and a bowl. "We're turning in for the night, but here's a bedtime snack for you boys—papaya juice and popped amaranth. Be sure to turn out the lights when you come upstairs."

The juice wasn't bad, but the amaranth looked as if it had been too pooped to pop. Brian dug right into it. We watched an old black-and-white cowboy movie. I fell asleep about halfway into it.

I was dreaming about riding a horse across
the plains when suddenly the horse began
bucking and jumping. It was Brian shaking
me. "Josh! Wake up! This is what we can do
for our project."

"Do what?" I mumbled, trying to figure out
where I was. Brian pushed up his glasses on

his nose and pointed to the TV screen. "I just watched this guy hypnotize a whole bunch of people. It looks easy. I've been taking notes."

I headed for the stairs.

"Hey, where are you going?"

"To bed. There's no way I'm going to let you hypnotize me. I'd rather get a D in science."

Brian held up his hands. "No, wait. I wasn't going to hypnotize you."

I stopped by the stairs. "Well I only see two people in the room, and if you're the hypnotist, that makes me the person who's getting out of here."

"There are three people in this room," Brian said. He jerked his head toward the corner where Arful was snoring softly.

"Arful? You're going to hypnotize the dog?"

Brian motioned for me to come closer. "I have to get some stuff ready first, so we'll do it tomorrow," he whispered. "I'm going to make Arful think he's a cat. I'll bet nobody has ever done that before."

"You're going to make a dog think he's a cat?"

"Shhhhh! If he knows what we're trying to do, he might just be pretending to be a cat. Then we wouldn't know if he was really hypnotized or not."

That's the thing about Brian. Sometimes he's a genius and sometimes he's a pea brain. But that's what makes him interesting.

And that's what always gets me into trouble.

CHAPTER TWO

Mrs. Lewis was in her usual form for breakfast. "Here's a nice big dish of granola with prune yogurt, Josh." She held out a bowl of gray and purple stuff.

I didn't have much choice about eating it, or at least pretending to eat it. Mom says when you're a guest in somebody's house, you should be polite and eat the food they serve you. At least three bites of it. When I tried it, it tasted a lot better than it looked—sort of like Frooty-O's cereal mushed up in milk.

"It's my day to volunteer at the natural

foods co-op, Brian. You'll be here with your father. I'm sure you'll remember to be quiet when he has patients in his office."

"We will, Mom."

Mrs. Lewis smiled. "What are your plans for the day, boys?"

"We're working on a project for the science fair," Brian said.

Mrs. Lewis's smile got even bigger. "That's wonderful. What's the project? Not that I'm prying, you understand. I know some parents practically do their children's school projects for them, but you know how your father and I feel about letting you exercise your own creativity."

Brian nodded solemnly. "I know, Mom. We're doing an experiment in . . . dog training."

"How exciting, dear. I'm sure you'll do a wonderful job. Heaven knows, Arful needs some training. Just make sure you don't hurt his feelings. He's rather sensitive, you know. I wouldn't want him to feel he was underachieving."

"We won't, Mom."

She threw a kiss and left.

"Your mother is worried about Arful underachieving," I said. "The only thing he knows how to do is eat, sleep, and breathe. He'd have to drop dead to achieve any less."

"Arful is a thinker, not a doer," Brian said. "That's what makes him a perfect subject."

The minute Dr. Lewis went into his office with his first patient, Brian starting searching through the videotapes in the family room.

"I thought we were going to work on the project," I said. "We have to hand in our plan on Monday, you know." It wasn't that I loved to do homework on the weekend. I just knew I wasn't going to come up with any great ideas on my own.

"This *is* for our project." Brian pulled out a video and slipped it in the VCR. The screen filled with the face of a cat and the words *The Mysterious World of the Cat.*

"What's this supposed to prove?"

"Before we can hypnotize Arful into thinking he's a cat, we have to understand how a cat acts." He handed me a blank notebook and a pencil. "Here. We'll both take notes."

The video lasted for an hour. When it was over, Brian had filled up half of his notebook. I had one page. It said, *The Mysterious World of the Cat.*

When we went upstairs, Brian stopped at his parents' door. "Take Arful into my room," he said. "I'll be right there."

When he came back, he was winding one of his mother's long purple scarves around his head. Then he fastened it in the front with a fancy jeweled pin.

"What are you supposed to be?"

"This is the way the guy dressed on TV, remember? It helps set the mood." He studied his notebook for a minute. "Okay. Let's pick out the first cat traits for the training session." He read through his list. "I think we ought to do the sense of smell and purring." He pushed up his glasses and looked at me. "Pick something from your list."

I flipped through my empty notebook, trying to think of what was catlike about our cat, Marmalade. "How about fish?"

"What about fish? I don't remember that from the video."

"It wasn't in the video. I'm talking from experience. Marmalade loves fish. Her cat food stinks! I don't know how she eats that stuff. And Mom has to make sure she can't get to the fish in our aquarium. She sits on the floor and watches them."

"Fish." Brian scribbled in his notebook. "That's good. We'll test Arful to see if he'll eat fish, then we'll take him over to your house to look at the aquarium. Now hold him still."

I sat next to Arful and put my arm around his neck. With both of us sitting down, he was taller than me. He leaned down to lick my ear, but lost interest when he didn't find any chicken grease on it.

Brian sat cross-legged in front of us. He held up a gold chain with a big crystal hanging from it. "You are getting *sleeeeepy*," he said, swinging it back and forth.

"Of course I'm sleepy. You kept me up half the night."

"Are you going to help me, or are you just going to make smart remarks?"

"Make smart remarks," I said.

Brian stood up. "All right. I'll call Emily Venable. She'll be glad to be my partner."

Brian was right. Emily would come trotting over here in a second to team up with him. She'd had a crush on Brian since first grade. But if I didn't stick with Brian, I wouldn't get to see if he could really hypnotize his dog. And I didn't have any better ideas for the science fair. Most important of all, I needed an A.

"All right," I said. "Let's get this over with."

Brian came closer and started swinging the crystal. Arful watched it for about half a minute. Then he chomped down on the crystal, pulling it right out of Brian's hand. I grabbed the end of the chain just before it slipped through his slobbery lips.

"Why did you let him do that?" Brian yelled. "You were supposed to be holding him!"

"Hold him! Your dog weighs as much as a school bus!"

"My mother will kill me. This is a special crystal that cures headaches."

"At least Arful won't get any more headaches," I said.

Brian grabbed his dog around the neck. "You pry open his jaws, and I'll pull out the chain."

The second I even touched Arful's jaws, he let out a growl that sounded like thunder. I let go. "How about *you* pry open his jaws? He's your dog."

"This isn't going to work," Brian said. "We have to distract him. Just keep hanging on to the end of the chain while I go get something for him to eat."

Arful and I sat staring at each other. I could feel little tugs on the chain as he worked the crystal around in his mouth. The whole time, he was quietly growling deep in his throat, just to let me know who was in charge. But as soon as Brian ran back in and held a bagel in front of his nose, Arful opened his mouth. I yanked the crystal out.

First we had to wait until Arful had licked all the garlic bits off the bagel. Then we had to wait about twenty minutes until he finished eating it. Arful was old, with bad teeth. He didn't chew his food. He licked it to death.

"Okay," Brian said finally. "Get in your positions."

"Arful doesn't even know 'sit and stay.' You think he understands 'get in your positions'?"

"Just do it," Brian said. He was losing patience.

This time Brian sat farther away. I hooked my arm tight around Arful's shoulders and gripped my hands together against his hairy chest. His warm breath was a combination of garlic and bad dog teeth. At first, Arful just moved his head back and forth, watching the swinging crystal, but pretty soon his whole body was swaying from side to side, taking me with him.

"You are getting *sleeeeepy*. Your eyelids are getting heavy . . . very heavy. You want to close your eyes and go to sleep."

Pretty soon the crystal got all blurry. Then there were two crystals swinging next to each other. Arful and I swayed. I felt all warm and cozy, like a baby being rocked in a cradle. I just leaned my head on Arful's soft shoulder and watched the blurry crystals.

"You are a *caaaaat*," Brian's voice droned. "When you are happy, you purr."

Back and forth went the crystals. Back and forth.

"You are a *caaaaaaat*. You have an acute sense of smell. You can smell things from a great distance away."

Swing . . . swing . . . swing.

"You are a *caaaaaaaat*. You would rather eat fish than anything else in the whole world. And you like to watch them in an aquarium." Back and forth went the crystals. Back and forth and back and . . . zzzzzzzzz.

CHAPTER THREE

"**W**hen I snap my fingers, you will wake up as a cat."

SNAP!

"Hey, Josh! I think it worked."

"What worked?" I mumbled. What was Brian doing in my room in the middle of the night?

"The hypnosis worked. Did you see how Arful's eyes got all glazed over?"

"Arful's eyes?"

"Wait here. I'm going to get something to

make the first test." Brian slammed out of the room and ran downstairs. I blinked and looked around. I was in Brian's room, not mine. Then I remembered about the sleepover and the science fair project.

Brian came running back into the room with Arful's food dish. Arful gobbled it in a couple of gulps, then licked the dish until it was shiny with dog drool. Brian grabbed his clipboard and marked something down. "Arful passed the first test. He ate the anchovies."

"Anchovies? Those gross little fish that my Dad always orders on pizzas?"

"Yep. Glommed them right down. He's already starting to act like a cat."

"Come on, Brian, Arful would eat dirty gym socks. I don't think this proves he thinks he's a cat."

Brian frowned, sending his glasses sliding down his nose. "That's why the fish test has two parts. Now we take him over to your house to see if he shows any interest in the fish in your aquarium."

We had to wait until Dr. Lewis came out of the office between patients to get permission to leave. Then we went to find Arful. He was curled up on the couch in the family room.

Brian grabbed my arm. "Do you hear that?"

"What?"

"The purring. Arful is purring!"

"You sure that's not just snoring?"

"Look at the expression on his face, Josh. He's practically smiling. Cats purr when they're happy. This is going to be the easiest A we ever got."

"Okay," I said. "Write it down and let's get going."

Brian woke Arful up and we headed out.

Halfway to my house, we ran into Emily. "Hi, Brian," she cooed. "Taking your dog for a walk?"

"We're working on our science project," he said.

"What a coincidence. That's what I'm doing, too." Emily held up a bunch of weeds. "I'm gathering wild herbs. My partner is Lissa Franken, but she had to go to her grandmother's this weekend, so I have to do this part all by myself. Do you have a partner, Brian?"

"What am I, invisible?" I said. "You don't see two people standing here?"

Emily noticed me. "Oh, I just thought Brian would pick someone more . . . more . . . interested in school for his science project partner." She smiled a fake little smile. "No offense, Josh."

Brian didn't even stick up for me. He was busy watching Arful, who was busy watching a robin, who was busy watching a worm squirming in somebody's driveway. Then Arful dove for the bird, dragging Brian halfway down the street before the robin flew off. Brian was already scribbling in his notebook when I caught up to them. "Did you see how he acted? Chasing birds? Was that catlike, or what?"

"I don't want to burst your little bubble here, Brian, but that doesn't mean Arful thinks he's a cat."

"Why not?"

"Well, was that part of the hypnosis? You told him he'd like fish, but did you mention anything about chasing birds?"

Brian looked at me for a second, pushed his glasses up his nose, then erased what he had written in his notebook. "You're right, Josh. I'm seeing what I want to see, not making scientific observations. Nice catch."

That made me feel pretty good. Maybe Brian wasn't the only smart person on this team. When we got to my house, we took Arful right to the aquarium.

"He sees the fish," Brian said.

"Yeah, but he doesn't look very excited about them." That surprised me, because they were pretty interesting to watch.

"That's because his hair is in his eyes." Brian picked up one of my sister's barrettes from the coffee table. "This ought to fix it." He grabbed a hunk of Arful's hair and clipped it back to the top of his head.

Just then, Mom came in from the kitchen. "Interesting hairdo on the dog, Brian. Is he trying to grow out his bangs?"

"We're doing an experiment, Mrs. Buckner. I just thought Arful could see better with the hair out of his eyes."

Mom ran her fingers through my hair. "I keep telling Josh that, but he bolts every time I pull out the Hairvac."

"What's a Hairvac?" Brian asked.

"Haven't you ever seen it?" Before I could stop Mom, she was pulling the machine out of the closet. "This is the greatest invention in the world, Brian. It's a hair cutter that attaches to your vacuum cleaner. Sit down, Josh. We'll give Brian a demonstration."

"Aw, Mom!" Before I could get away, she shoved me into a kitchen chair and plugged the thing in. "The vacuum cleaner sucks up the hair," she shouted over the roar, "then, the little blades in the Hairvac cut the hair off evenly. It's neat, too. All the cut hair just gets whisked away." You'd think she was doing a TV commercial.

"Yeah, real neat!" I grumbled, feeling my scalp tingle where my hair was being vacuumed.

"Could you do that on Arful?" Brian shouted to Mom.

"I don't know why not," Mom yelled back. "I'll Hairvac him as soon as I finish up with Josh."

"If you think you're ever getting that thing on me again after you use it on that mangy dog, I'll . . ."

Mom shut off the vacuum, leaving my voice bellowing across the kitchen. "You'll what?" she said, running her fingers through what was left of my hair.

I felt a draft on my neck. "You always cut it too short."

"That's because you hardly ever let me cut it. Once I get my hands on you, the cut has to last for several months. Okay, next customer."

Brian and I struggled to lift Arful into the chair. "I'd better earn his trust before I turn on the vacuum," Mom said. "I wish I had some dog biscuits. I guess kitty treats will have to do."

Marmalade came dashing into the kitchen when she heard the treat cupboard open.

Then she saw Arful and tried to stop, but her paws slipped on the waxed floor. She kept skidding forward, even though she was back-pedaling like crazy. She hit the stove like a runner sliding into home base, then gathered her feet under her and streaked out of the room. It all happened so fast, Arful didn't even see her. He was concentrating on the kitty treats that Mom was feeding him.

"He seems to like these," Mom said. "Maybe your dog thinks he's a cat, Brian."

Brian glanced my way. He didn't smile, but he was wiggling his eyebrows so hard, they looked like two caterpillars wrestling on his forehead.

"You know, Brian," Mom said, "before I start the haircut, we should call your mother and ask if it's all right."

"I know she wouldn't mind, Mrs. Buckner. She's been talking about getting a haircut for him. You'd be saving her a lot of money."

Mom fed Arful another kitty treat. "Well, if you're sure, I guess it's all right." By the time Mom started Hairvaccing Arful, the dog was

in love with her. He didn't even flinch when she turned on the vacuum and the hair on the top of his head stood on end. Pretty soon he had a nice spike haircut, but when she turned off the vacuum, the hair flopped back into his face. Mom stood across the room and squinted at Arful. "The way I see it, you have two choices—a shorter cut or mousse."

"Make it shorter, Mrs. Buckner. Real short. A buzz. I know that's what Mom wants him to have."

"Coming right up," Mom said, turning on the machine.

I shouted into Brian's ear. "Your mom doesn't know anything about this. Isn't she going to be mad when she sees Arful?"

"Not when I tell her we did it because he couldn't see very well," he shouted back. "That's just being humane. Besides, did you ever see a cat with hair in its eyes? Even the long-haired Persians have short hair on top."

The thing about cutting hair is knowing when to stop. Arful looked funny with the hair just short on top, so Mom tried to even it

up by cutting the sides. Then he looked like this big hairy dog with a peanut head, so we all decided she should give him a trim on the shoulders, back, and chest. But then he looked like he had this fat belly, and when she trimmed that, he looked like a poodle with big puffy legs. I told her to keep going, because I thought Arful's haircut would kill off the Hairvac for good. But the Hairvac was still going strong when Arful had hair a half-inch long all over his body, and the vacuum cleaner was coughing up hairballs.

CHAPTER FOUR

Monday morning, Mrs. Metz let us talk with our partners about our science projects as she came around to our desks to hear our plans. Brian had typed our plan on his father's computer. He used a lot of big words.

"Is that how you spell hypnosis?" I asked, trying to sound out the word. "It looks like hypo . . . hypoth . . ."

"Not hypnosis. Hypothesis," Brian said. "It states what we're trying to prove."

"Which is what, exactly?"

"It tells you right here, Josh. 'We think it is possible to train a dog to think he's a cat.'"

"Then where does it say anything about the hypnosis?"

Brian shrugged. "I didn't mention it. I'm not sure that hypnosis is a true science. My father says the psychiatrists who use hypnosis are quacks."

"Oh, that's just great, Brian. Then our whole experiment is stupid?"

"Shhhh! Mrs. Metz will hear you. I said my father thinks hypnosis is for quacks. But I'm telling you, Josh, I saw it work with my own eyes on that TV show."

"Well, it isn't working very well on Arful."

"We don't know that for sure. Besides, we have three whole weeks to keep hypnotizing him. I'm calling it 'training' on our project plan, just to be on the safe side."

Just then, Mrs. Metz reached our desk. "I hope you boys don't mind, but after the class divided into pairs, we had one extra student. I'd like him to join your team."

"Sure, Mrs. Metz," Brian said, all dreamy-eyed. He had a crush on Mrs. Metz and would probably even take Dougie Hanks as a partner, if she asked him to.

Mrs. Metz smiled, making the dimples show in her cheeks. "Thanks, boys. I knew you wouldn't mind." She turned toward the back of the room. "Dougie! Bring your chair over here."

I couldn't believe it. Brian didn't even seem to notice that the stupidest kid in the class was joining our team. He was too busy smiling at Mrs. Metz.

Dougie dragged his chair over. When he plunked down in it, my foot was underneath. "Ow!" I yelled. "Watch what you're doing, Dougie. I think you broke my toe!" Dougie's hair always hung down in his eyes, so he couldn't see where he was going.

"Uh, sorry," Dougie mumbled. He moved the chair and flopped down in it again.

Mrs. Metz picked up Brian's paper. "Let's see what you boys have planned. Hmmm. 'Hypothesis'—good word, boys."

Brian grinned and turned as red as his shirt.

She frowned a little as she read on. "You think you can train a dog to think he's a cat?

That sounds like a . . . difficult project. Maybe you should think of something . . . easier."

Dougie snorted. "That's the dumbest idea I ever heard of. Why can't we make one of them volcanoes out of that mashed paper stuff?"

I hated hearing my idea coming out of Dougie's mouth. "We don't want an easy project, Mrs. Metz," I said. "We want a challenge. Besides, we started this weekend, and it's working already."

Mrs. Metz smiled. Her dimples were really getting a workout. "Well, if you have your hearts set on this project, I don't want to discourage you. We have someone else doing dog training, but this is certainly the most original idea I've ever seen. Just don't be disappointed if you can't prove your hypothesis."

"Prove what?" Dougie asked.

"Brian and Josh will explain it to you, Dougie. I hope you enjoy working together."

"Yeah, okay," Dougie mumbled. Mrs. Metz moved on to the next team. Dougie stood up and dragged his chair back to his desk. So much for teamwork.

Emily rushed right over, wide-eyed. "Is Dougie on your team, Brian?"

Brian nodded, just beginning to realize we were stuck with him.

"Oh, you poor thing. I'd try to switch with him, but I know Lissa wouldn't be caught dead working with Dougie. Besides," she rolled her eyes, "I've done all the work so far on our project, and Lissa gets half of the credit. But of course," she looked right at me, "you know what that's like, don't you, Brian?" She gave him a little pat on the shoulder and went back to her seat.

At lunch that day, Dougie Hanks came to sit at our table. "Just because you're on our science fair team doesn't mean you have to hang out with us, Dougie," I said.

Dougie slid in next to me. "That's okay. I don't mind." He pulled a piece of cold pizza out of his lunch bag and started chewing the stretchy cheese off the top of it.

I unwrapped my sandwich. Peanut butter again. Boring! Just then, I sniffed something interesting in the air. "I'll be right back," I said, following my nose. It led me right to Kamiko Osaka. She was arranging some thick disk-shaped things about the size of fifty-cent pieces on her napkin.

"What are you having for lunch, Kamiko?"

"Sushi. Why?"

"What's in it?"

"Raw fish, mostly. Why?"

"How would you like to trade for a peanut butter and jelly?"

She snatched the sandwich from my hand and shoved the sushi across the table. "It's a deal! My mother never buys peanut butter, and nobody ever wants to trade for sushi."

"I will!" I said. "Anytime you want!"

When I got back to the table with my treasure, Brian made a face. "If you wanted to trade lunches, even mine is better than that."

I took a bite. "This stuff just happens to be delicious."

"Better than veggie burger on twelve-grain bread?" Brian offered. He never got to trade lunches, either.

"You guys eat weird," Dougie said. He wolfed down the last of his cold pizza.

That afternoon after school, Brian and I followed Arful around, trying to observe cat-like behavior. Dougie was supposed to come too, but he never showed up. We got caught in the rain and had to duck under a tree until it let up. Then the sun came out and it turned really hot and humid. We trailed Arful until he flopped down on Brian's front porch.

"See what he's doing now?" Brian asked, pulling out his notebook.

"What? Panting?"

"Not panting. He's smelling."

"What does that prove? He always smells when he's wet."

"Not smelly. Smelling." Brian flipped through the pages of his notebook. "Here it is, under *Acute Sense of Smell.* The cat has a secondary sense organ inside his mouth. When he looks like he's panting, he's really trying to catch a faint scent."

"Okay," I said. I wasn't going to argue with Brian, but I was pretty sure Arful was panting . . . and smelly!

CHAPTER FIVE

That Friday, Brian invited Dougie to sleep over for the next part of our project. This time, he showed up. First thing he did was make fun of Arful. "What kind of a dog is that? Looks like he got a bad haircut."

Arful was curled up quietly—almost cat-like—in the corner.

Mrs. Lewis's lips twitched, then she managed a faint smile. "I'm sure Arful will look fine when it grows out."

Dougie's mouth fell open. "Whoa! It really was a haircut? I was only kidding, Mrs. Lewis.

I thought maybe he was just one of them ugly dogs. You oughta go get your money back, Mrs. Lewis. I'd sue the guy who did that, if I was you. Honest!"

I started pushing Dougie toward the stairs. "Now that you're here, Dougie, we can get busy on our science fair project." I didn't want to remind Mrs. Lewis how mad she was at Mom for Arful's Hairvaccing. She told Brian that if it wasn't for the science fair, he wouldn't be allowed to come to my house anymore.

Brian figured out what I was doing. "Yeah, right." He grabbed Arful by the collar. "We have a lot to do, so we'd better get started."

"I'll bring up some snacks for you in a little while," Mrs. Lewis said.

Brian stopped on the stairs and turned to her. "No, thanks, Mom. It's very important that Arful gives us his full attention. We can't have any interruptions, especially with food. You know how he is."

Brian closed the door to his room, pulled the scarf out from a dresser drawer, and started wrapping it around his head.

"What are you doing, playing dress up?" Dougie asked.

"I'm going to hypnotize Arful," Brian said, pulling out his mother's crystal. "You can help Josh hold him."

Dougie snorted. "Yeah, right! So what are you doing, really?"

I got in my position beside Arful. "Listen, Dougie. This is a serious project. If you don't want to help, you can go home right now."

"I'm in," Dougie said, sitting on the other side of Arful. "I don't want to miss this."

"Then wipe that stupid grin off your face," I said.

Brian started the crystal swinging. "You are getting *sleeeeepy*. Very, very *sleeeepy*. You can hardly keep your eyes open. You are . . . I can't do this with you grinning at me, Dougie."

With that, Dougie snorted and collapsed on the floor. "You should see yourself in that stupid hat . . . and that creepy voice . . . this is better than TV!"

"That's it!" Brian said. "Go sit on the bed and keep quiet. You're going to bring my mother up here. We don't need your help, anyway. We're just doing you a favor letting you be on our team."

Dougie sat on the bed. He was still grinning.

"You are getting *sleeeeepy*. Your eyelids are getting heavy."

The crystal was blurry already. Arful and I swayed in rhythm. He seemed to remember what he was supposed to do.

"You are a *caaaaaat,*" Brian droned.

There was a snort and explosion from the bed. "And you guys are supposed to be the class brains? I wonder what the class idiots are doing!"

"One of them is watching us, and he's going to be kicked off the team if he doesn't wise up," Brian said, without turning around. Then he fell right back into his chanting. "You are a *caaaaaat.*"

Class brains? Dougie thought I was a class brain? Maybe compared to him, I was. The crystal was in focus again. Then Arful started swaying and it blurred and became two.

"You are good at hunting. You love to catch mice."

Swing . . . sway . . . warm and blurry.

"You are stealthy. You walk by moving both of your right feet then both of your left feet."

Crystals . . . pretty . . . sparkle . . . swing.

"You have an acute sense of hearing. You

45

can hear a mouse walking through a wall. Your ears swivel around to catch the sound. You can hear one and a half octaves higher than a human."

Nice . . . swaying . . . swinging . . . warm.

"When I snap my fingers, you will wake up." SNAP!

I blinked. I felt as if I had just gotten out of a warm bath and wrapped myself up in a big fuzzy towel. Then Dougie's snorting brought the room back into focus.

Brian unwound his turban. "Don't think I couldn't hear you, Dougie, laughing the whole time."

"You didn't hear me laughing. What you heard was me trying *not* to laugh. Besides, what do you expect? You're dressed up like my Aunt Ella, and Josh and the dog look like a couple of drunks. Don't even *think* about winning the Wonderland Lake passes. We're getting an F on this project for sure."

"That's how much you know," I said. "We're going to do something that's never been done before."

Dougie shrugged. "It's all the same to me, because I'll get an F either way. But you guys are used to getting A's." He yawned. "I'm beat. See you in the morning." He hunkered down into his sleeping bag and was asleep in about a minute and a half.

Brian looked as if he'd been kicked in the stomach. He'd probably never thought about not getting an A.

"Don't worry, Brian," I whispered. "Dougie's a jerk. What does he know, anyway? This project is going to win the science fair."

"I'm not so sure."

"Well I am. Let's get some sleep, and we'll test Arful in the morning. I bet he's at least half cat already."

I climbed into Brian's extra bed and punched the pillow until it was just the way I liked it. Then I stayed awake half the night listening to the ticking of the grandfather clock down in the living room. I'd never noticed before how loud it was.

CHAPTER SIX

After breakfast, we all took Arful outside. He walked around the backyard a few times, then flopped down in the sun. He used to nap under a tree, but since his haircut he seemed to want to be where it was warm.

"So what happens now?" Dougie asked.

Brian pulled his notebook out of his pocket. "We're making scientific observations."

"Of what?" Dougie asked. "We're gonna watch your dog sleep?"

"There," Brian said. "Did you see that? He just swiveled his ear to hear something."

"His ear had a fly on it," Dougie said. "Pretty soon he'll probably scratch it."

Brian glared at Dougie. "I think I know a swivel when I see it."

Dougie just grinned and pointed at Arful, who was scratching his ear.

Brian rubbed out what he had written and blew away the eraser crumbs. "All right, let's see if he's walking like a cat yet. Here, Arful. Come here, boy."

Arful got up and stretched, then walked slowly across the yard, his head drooping.

"That," said Brian, "is what I call stealthy walking."

"I don't know about stealthy," said Dougie, "but he sure isn't getting nowhere fast."

Brian was scribbling furiously in his notebook. "Stealthy means slow and deliberate. That's what he's doing. He's probably stalking something."

Dougie wouldn't give up. "What about that stuff you said in the hypnosis—that he was supposed to move both of his right legs together, then both of his left legs? He isn't doing that."

"So what?" I said. I was sick of Dougie challenging everything Brian said. "Who cares what order he moves his feet in?"

"Dougie's right, Josh. The cat is the only animal who walks that way, except for the giraffe."

Dougie snorted. "Maybe we can stretch out his neck and make him think he's a giraffe. Couldn't be any harder than this cat thing."

Brian got down on his hands and knees beside Arful. "Maybe he just needs to get the feel of it. Josh, you take his right legs and I'll take his left ones."

"Aw, Brian."

"Just do it!"

I hunkered down and took hold of Arful's legs.

"Here we go," Brian said. "Right legs first."

"This is like trying to move a tank. I can't budge him."

Brian sighed. "All right. I'll go first." He heaved on Arful's legs and the dog tipped over, right on my head.

Dougie was rolling on the ground, laughing so hard that he only made little squeaking sounds.

Arful scrambled to get his footing and almost clawed my ear off. Brian helped me up. "Sorry, Josh. I guess that was a dumb idea."

Dougie finally got his voice back. "You know, I always thought doing homework was boring, but with you guys, it's better than going to a movie. What's next?"

Brian flipped the pages of his notebook. "Well, we could test him on catching mice . . . if we had any mice."

"We have a whole bunch of them in our barn," Dougie said. "You want to come over?"

Brian looked at me. I tried to signal "no" without actually shaking my head. He didn't get it. "Sure," he said. "Why not?"

Brian asked his dad if he could go, and I called home to let Mom know. Dougie lived about five blocks away, just where the edge of town gave way to farmland.

Arful seemed scared of his own shadow on the way over. "Do you see how his personality has changed?" Brian asked. "In the old days, he would have been dragging us along. Now he's spooked by every little noise. It must be his new acute sense of hearing. Probably everything seems loud to him."

"Everything is loud out here," I said. "The traffic and all."

Dougie was trailing behind us. "Hey, Josh! Why are you walking funny?"

"I'm not."

"Yeah, you are. It's the way you're swinging your arms. Like Frankenstein."

I turned around and glared at Dougie. After that, I couldn't stop thinking about how my arms were swinging. Every move I made seemed clumsy. Finally I just stuck my hands in my pockets.

Dougie lived on an old farm with wrecks of cars and a tractor with two flat tires in the field. He headed right for the barn.

"Don't you have to tell your parents you're here?" I asked.

Dougie shrugged. "Nah. Probably nobody's home."

Brian's mouth dropped open. "You can have people over when nobody's home?"

"Sure. It's only me and Aunt Ella here and she don't care what I do, as long as I don't set the house on fire or nothing."

Brian looked around. "Is this a real farm with animals and everything?"

"Used to be," Dougie said. "When my grandpa was alive, he had a whole dairy herd. Now we just have a few chickens for eggs is all."

The only light in the barn was from a hole in the roof. Three cats scattered when we came in, stirring up dust that floated in the beam of sunlight. Arful was so spooked, we practically had to drag him into the barn. Brian finally got him calmed down and motioned for me and Dougie to sit on some bales of hay and be quiet.

Arful looked around the barn, his eyes wide.

"I think he hears mice," Brian said. "Look. He's crouching. He's stalking something."

Sure enough, Arful was sinking to the floor.

Brian pulled out his notebook. "He's doing it. Listen to this. 'The hunting behavior of the domestic cat. Number one. Flattens body to ground.'"

"Check," I said.

Brian marked it in the notebook. "'Number two. Glides closer to prey.'"

"Cats pray?" asked Dougie. "Where'd you hear that?"

"*P-R-E-Y,* not pray, hummingbird brain," I said. "Prey is what he's hunting. Glides closer to the mouse."

"Oh." Dougie nodded. "But he's not moving."

Brian was already checking it off. "He's moving very slowly. You have to be really observant to see it. There's number three. 'Crouches to watch prey.'" He checked it off.

"Your dog's crouching looks just like his gliding."

"Aha!" Brian whispered, ignoring Dougie. "'Number four. Twitches tail.'"

"Yeah," Dougie said. "I saw that."

Brian flipped the page of his notebook, scribbling like mad. Then he squinted hard at Arful. "There's number five—'Sways head from side to side.' If I wasn't watching for it, I would have missed it."

"You're nuts," Dougie said. "That dog couldn't move any less if he was dead."

Brian shook his notebook in Dougie's face. "I'm sick and tired of you putting down everything we're doing. This is a serious project. Have you ever heard of scientific observation?"

"Sure," Dougie said. "Have you ever heard of *The Emperor's New Clothes*?"

Leave it to Dougie to make a dumb remark. He'd look really stupid when Arful caught his first mouse, which should be any second now, because I could hear little mouse feet running all through the hay bales.

CHAPTER SEVEN

Back in school on Monday, each team had to stand up and say how its project was coming along. A lot of kids were doing pretty dumb stuff. There were five teams making volcanoes, three doing tornadoes in a bottle, and eight teams making solar systems. Only one other team was doing dog training. Tony Alessi and Chad Dawes were teaching their dogs to go through an obstacle course.

"We'll need a lot of space to set up the course for Parents' Night," Chad said. "Maybe even our own separate room."

"Well, even though you have a very interesting project," Mrs. Metz said, "you can't count on being one of the teams chosen for Parents' Night."

Chad turned red. "Oh, yeah, well, I know, but, just in case . . . ." You could tell he still thought they were going to win.

"You all will have table space to display your projects in the cafeteria," Mrs. Metz said, "but our three class winners will give their demonstrations up on the stage. All of the teams should make sure their projects will fit into that space."

"Oh we will, Mrs. Metz," Chad said. "Just in case we happen to win, I mean." Yeah, right.

Then it was Emily's turn. "Lissa and I are doing 'Herbs and Their Many Uses.' We have looked up some delicious recipes to show how herbs are used in cooking." She smiled at Mrs. Metz. "We'll be bringing samples for the judges at Parents' Night . . . if we're one of the finalists. I'm describing all of the dishes in our written report."

I knew we were in trouble now. There was nothing our principal, Mr. Purvis, liked more than food. He'd vote for Emily to be one of the three finalists, just so he could eat her samples.

When it was our turn, Brian did the talking. "We are training my dog to act like a cat. So far, it's going very well."

Dougie snorted.

Brian glared at him. "Well, it is."

"Tell how many mice your dog caught," Dougie said.

Brian frowned. "Not all cats are good mousers. Some of them have become so domesticated and used to canned cat food that they . . ."

"How many mice?" Dougie insisted.

Brian whirled around. "No mice, okay? But how do we know there were any mice in your barn in the first place? Your cats probably ate them all."

Mrs. Metz came over and put her hands on Dougie's shoulders. "Now, boys, remember

you're a team. You should work together and respect one another's opinions. You'll be handing in your written observations a week from today, and that's what you'll be judged on."

How could we respect the opinions of the dumbest kid in the class? All we could hope for was the fact that Brian was so good at writing, he might make our project sound really great, even if it wasn't.

We were back at Brian's the next Saturday morning for the final hypnosis. At least Brian and I were there. Dougie hadn't shown up yet. Brian's mother was out of town and his father was in his office with a patient. "Come on," Brian said. "Let's go up to my room and get started."

"But don't we have to wait for Dougie? I mean, I don't want to, but he's supposed to be doing this with us."

Brian scratched Arful behind the ears. "Nothing says Dougie has to be here for the hypnosis. He just laughs through the whole thing, anyway."

"Yeah, but what if he comes right in the middle and messes everything up?"

"He won't. I told him we were starting at 10:30. That gives us a half hour."

"Good thinking! Let's go!"

Brian had his turban wrapped and pinned with the jewel when the doorbell rang. "You answer it, Josh. I don't want to have to do the turban all over again."

"Won't your father get it?"

"He's not going to run out on his patient and answer the door. It's probably just somebody selling something. Tell them we don't want any."

The doorbell was ringing like crazy. I ran downstairs to answer it. It was Dougie. "You're early."

"Our clock is broke. So what if I'm early? You are, too."

"All right. Come on." I led Dougie up to Brian's room.

Brian looked surprised. "You're early."

"Maybe I got here just in time," Dougie said, flopping down on Brian's bed. "Unless you're wearing the fancy hat all the time now."

Brian ignored Dougie and got Arful and me set up. Then he pulled out the crystal and started in. "You are getting *sleeeepy*. Your eyelids are getting heavy."

The crystal only swung back and forth once before it blurred and split in two. Brian was getting really good at this. Arful and I rocked silently.

"You are very independent," Brian moaned. "You do what you want when you want to."

"You love catnip," Dougie echoed in a spooky voice.

"Cut it out, Dougie. I'm doing the hypnosis here."

The crystal came into sharp focus again.

"You're telling him stupid stuff," Dougie said. "How are we going to know if he's independent or not? You can't test that. You should be teaching him real cat stuff, not something you got from a book."

"And what makes you such an expert on cats?"

"We got a whole mess of cats in the barn, remember? I know how they act."

"You think you can do this better than me?"

Brian unwound the turban. "If you're so smart, you do it."

Dougie grabbed the scarf and wrapped it around his head. Then he took the crystal, sat down, and started it swinging. "You are getting *sleeeeeepy.*"

Instant fuzzy crystal. Two of them.

"You are a *caaaaat.* When you eat catnip, you get real stupid and roll all over the floor."

Swing . . . swing . . . swing.

"You are a *caaaat.* After you eat, you lick yourself all over to clean up."

Swing . . . swing . . . swing.

"You are a *caaat.* You spend a lot of time taking naps in the sun."

Swing . . . swing.

"You are a *caaat.* Sometimes you cough up hairballs."

"That's enough!" Brian said. "I'm taking over. There's nothing scientific about what you're doing." He grabbed the turban off Dougie's head. The two of them were rolling around on the floor trying to wrestle the crystal away from each other when Dr. Lewis knocked on the door and came in.

"You boys will have to stop playing now. You're coming with me, Brian. Your mother just called. Her car has broken down and she needs us to pick her up. I'll drop the other boys off on the way."

So much for finishing our science project. It didn't really matter now. Brian was about to ruin his streak of straight A's, and I knew I could forget about having a ride on Screaming Mimi any time soon.

CHAPTER EIGHT

We took our written project to school on Monday. I should say we took Brian's written project, because Dougie and I didn't have anything to do with it. I was right about Brian making our project sound great, though. He made it sound so good, I was pretty sure we had a chance to win.

"Did you really see Arful do all this stuff?" Dougie asked, leaning over Brian's desk.

"Sure. You were there. You saw me writing it down."

Dougie cracked his gum. "Yeah, but you're the only one who saw it."

"No, Brian's right," I said. "I saw it, too . . . most of it."

"Did Arful do any of my stuff over the weekend?" Dougie asked. "Like going nuts over catnip? That would be a perfect test. I know dogs don't like catnip. Lots of the other junk you have here could be either for a dog or a cat. The hairballs are good, too. Never saw a dog throw up a hairball."

Brian pushed up his glasses. "You don't think you really hypnotized Arful, do you?"

"Sure, why not?"

"It takes a little more than a turban and a crystal to do hypnosis."

"Oh, yeah? Like what?"

Brian stood up. "You wouldn't understand. Give me the report. I'm going to hand it in."

At lunch I did my usual peanut-butter-sandwich-for-sushi trade with Kamiko. Whatever kind of fish her mother had used was especially delicious. I licked my fingers and even my hands and arms to get the last bit of taste.

Brian gave me a funny look. "Use a napkin, will you? That's disgusting."

"Leave him alone," Dougie said. "Who made you the neatness police?" Dougie's lunch was an almost-empty jar of peanut butter. He was scooping it out with his fingers.

"One thing I don't understand," Dougie said. "Let's say everybody else in the class drops dead and we end up winning, which is the only way we could win, if you ask me."

"Nobody asked you," Brian muttered between bites of his carob-chip-whole-wheat cookie.

"Well, just say we do win. How are we going to show Arful acting like a cat when we're up on the stage? What's he going to do?"

"We'll worry about that when the time comes," Brian said. "Arful is acting more like a cat each day. He even looks like a cat now, except for the long pointy nose."

Dougie snorted. "He looks like a dog having a bad hair day."

When we got back to class after lunch, the sun was shining on my desk. It felt so warm and nice, I started to feel drowsy. Pretty soon, I put my head down and fell asleep. Mrs. Metz had to wake me up three times before the end of the afternoon. Once she felt my forehead. "Are you feeling all right, Josh? This isn't like you. Maybe I should send you to the nurse's office."

"I'm okay, Mrs. Metz. Just sleepy." I didn't feel sick, but I did notice I had a funny ticklish feeling in the back of my throat, as if I had eaten something fuzzy and it got caught there.

The next day we waited for the announcement. The teachers had met after school to decide the winners. Mrs. Metz picked up a big sealed envelope from her desk. "This will be as much of a surprise to me as it will to you, boys and girls. This is so exciting! I feel like a presenter at the Academy Awards."

Her dimples were flashing all over the place. I thought Brian was going to pass out.

Mrs. Metz pulled out a piece of paper. "Our three class finalist teams are . . ."

She looked around the room, just to keep us in suspense. "Emily Venable and Lissa Franken—*Herbs and Their Many Uses.*"

Emily tried to look surprised, but she wouldn't have won an Academy Award for that performance.

"The next team is Tony Alessi and Chad Dawes—*Training Dogs to Go Through an Obstacle Course.*" Tony and Chad jumped up and high-fived each other. Then Chad ran down his whole row, high-fiving anybody he could get his hands on.

"That means we didn't get it," I whispered to Brian. "Why would they pick two dog training experiments?"

"Why would they pick theirs instead of ours? Our idea is much more original." Brian sounded sure of himself, but he had chewed so hard on his pencil eraser, he had bent the metal into a little pointed cap.

"Our third and last team . . ." Mrs. Metz looked around the class again. If she waited any longer, she might be causing the first actual explosion of a human being. Brian practically had steam coming out of his ears.

"Our final team is Brian Lewis, Josh Buckner, and Dougie Hanks—*Training a Dog to Act Like a Cat.*"

"No way!" Dougie shouted from the back of the room. He came running up to our seats, pounding me so hard on the back, he almost knocked the breath out of me. "Hey, how about that?" he yelled. "Nobody dropped dead and we won anyway!"

CHAPTER NINE

It seemed like everybody in the whole school was there for Parents' Night. I usually didn't mind crowds, but tonight I wanted to run out of there and go climb a tree or something. Even though the front hall was jammed with people, Mom and I bumped right into Brian, Mrs. Lewis, and Arful.

"Hi, Melanie," Mom said to Mrs. Lewis. "How is Arful enjoying his new haircut?"

Mrs. Lewis glared at Mom and opened her mouth to say something, but Brian tugged on her sleeve. "Come on, Mom. You want to have a spot in the front row, don't you?"

"That's a good idea, Brian," my mom said. "Let's go in now and get seats together, Melanie."

"No!" I pulled Mom away from the auditorium door. That's all we'd need tonight—a big fight between Mom and Mrs. Lewis.

"Josh! Let go! What's the matter with you?"

"I . . . I don't want you to go yet."

Mom looked into my face. "Are you nervous about presenting your project, honey?"

"No, I'm . . . yes! Yes, that's it! I'm really scared, Mom."

"All right, Josh. I'll stay with you until it's time to go onstage. Why don't we look at some of the projects in the cafeteria? That will take your mind off things." Before I could stop her, she turned to Mrs. Lewis. "You go on ahead, Melanie. I'm going to stay with Josh for a bit."

Mrs. Lewis glared at Mom. "He's scarred for life, you know."

Mom looked puzzled. "Who? Josh?"

Mrs. Lewis's eyes narrowed. "You know perfectly well who I'm talking about, Cindy Buckner. It's Arful."

Mom dropped to her knees next to Arful and began running her fingers over his coat. "Oh, I'm so sorry, Melanie. I didn't think it was possible to cut skin with a Hairvac. The commercial said . . ."

Mrs. Lewis pulled Arful away from Mom. "I'm not talking about physical scars. I'm talking about emotional scars."

Mom stood up. "Wait a minute, let me get this straight. You're worried about the dog having *emotional* scars?"

"Mom!" I pulled her arm, but she shook out of my grip.

"He's devastated by his appearance," Mrs. Lewis said. "You can tell he's embarrassed."

"*Now* he's embarrassed?" Mom said. "He spent his whole life looking like an unmowed lawn with legs, and *now* he's embarrassed?"

I grabbed Mom's arm again and pulled her toward the cafeteria. This time it worked, because Brian was pushing his mom in the

75

opposite direction. They were still yelling at each other as I dragged Mom through the cafeteria door. Mom got loose from my grip and smoothed down the front of her blouse. "The nerve of that woman. I gave her dog the best haircut of his life."

"The only haircut of his life," I pointed out.

"Exactly!" Mom was still muttering to herself as we walked up and down the rows of tables. It took her three and a half rows to calm down.

Now it was my turn to get upset. The thought of getting up in front of all those people terrified me.

It wasn't just the parents of our grade. All the fourth and fifth graders and their parents were there, too. Even if Brian did all the talking, what would we do if Arful just sat there? What if everybody laughed at us?

"Hey, Josh! Wait up!" It was Dougie, barreling across the cafeteria with some old lady behind him. She was wearing a bright purple turban that looked a lot like Brian's hypnosis outfit, only she had a purple dress to match it. "This is my Aunt Ella," Dougie said, when they got to us. "This here's Josh and his mom."

I almost didn't recognize Dougie. His face had been scrubbed so clean, it was red and shiny and his hair was slicked straight back. It was the first time I'd ever seen his eyebrows.

"Hi, Ella," Mom said. "I'm Cindy Buckner.

Don't we know each other from somewhere?"

"Probably the Shop and Save. I work at the customer service counter."

"That's right! You let me charge my groceries last week when I'd left my wallet at home. I'm really grateful for that."

Aunt Ella smiled. "Well, you have an honest face, dearie." She put her arm around Dougie's shoulder. "Aren't you proud of our boys? I always knew Dougie was smart. 'Bout time he used that brain of his."

Dougie sort of blushed when his aunt said that. It seemed weird. I never thought about somebody being proud of Dougie.

Aunt Ella motioned for us to follow her over to the cafeteria line. She reached into a small freezer and handed ice cream cups to Mom and me. "These are supposed to be for after, but I know there's more than enough. We donated them from the Shop and Save."

"Thanks, Ella," Mom said. The two of them started talking while Dougie and I dug into our ice cream.

I lapped up the cool vanilla ice cream. It

was easy until I was almost finished, but then it was hard to get my tongue into the bottom of the cup.

Mom glanced over at me. "Josh! For heaven's sake, use a spoon."

"I like it better this way," I said.

Mom just shook her head and turned back to Dougie's aunt.

I licked the last of the ice cream from my fingers. Then I licked the side of my hand to get it nice and wet and rubbed it over my mouth. Dougie watched me. I licked my hand again, this time rubbing way up over the back of my right ear.

Dougie grinned. "You are a real weirdo, Josh."

I was licking my left hand now, making sure I got the other side of my face clean. "What? I'm just cleaning up. I don't want to go on stage with ice cream all over my face." I gave an extra swipe over my left ear, and finished up with another juicy lick and a good hard scrub over my nose. Dougie shook his head.

Just then there was an announcement over

the loudspeaker. "Will all of the finalists please come backstage? We're ready to begin. Third grade science fair teams will be giving their demonstrations first."

I could feel the hairs on the back of my neck stand up.

CHAPTER TEN

We found Brian backstage with Arful. "Where were you guys? I thought I was going to have to do this by myself."

"Do what?" I whispered. "What are we going to show about Arful being a cat? He just looks like a dog with a bad haircut."

Brian raised his eyebrows. "And whose fault is that?"

"Yours! You're the one who conned my mom into Hairvaccing him."

"And you're the one who told her to keep going until the poor dog was bald."

Dougie grabbed each of us by the arm. "Cut it out, you guys. We're supposed to go sit on the stage."

We took our places and Mr. Purvis started the program. First we had the kids from Mrs. Jordan's class. Two girls had a big tube with earthworms in it. Each day they had turned the tube over to see if the earthworms would climb up toward the light. They read off the results—how many days the worms climbed to the top and how many days they dug to the bottom. It turned out to be about equal, so they decided the worms didn't much care one way or the other.

Then there were two boys with a parakeet. They had been teaching it to say "pretty bird," but all the bird would do was peck at the microphone. The noise sounded like explosions were going off all over the stage, and the whole audience started laughing. That spooked the bird so much, it flew right out of the kid's hand. It perched on one of the poles that were holding up the stage curtains.

Dougie leaned over and whispered. "I never came to a Parents' Night before. I didn't know they were this much fun."

The next project was two girls with some bugs in jars. You couldn't hear what they were saying, because they kept forgetting to talk into the mike. You could hear the parakeet, though. It was squawking, "Pretty bird, pretty bird," from above the stage.

Our class was next, and Emily and Lissa went first. They made everything a big deal, setting up a table and bringing out all of their dishes of food. Lissa held up bunches of dried weeds, while Emily lifted the cover off each dish and described how each herb was used in it. Then they scooped out samples for the judges. If everybody took this long, I figured we'd be there all night.

When we thought they were through, Emily started in again. "But herbs aren't just for cooking. Some are used as medicine." Then she went through a long list of herbs and what each one could cure. I was falling asleep until she reached down into a bag and pulled out the last of her weeds. "Some herbs are used by animals," she said. "This is catnip. It's like a tonic for cats; it makes them real frisky." Then she held up a little toy mouse. "This is my cat's favorite toy, a catnip mouse."

I looked over at Arful to see if he seemed interested, but he wasn't paying attention. I was surprised, because even I could smell it from this far away.

Chad and Tony were supposed to go next, but they had left something for their obstacle course in the Alessis' car, and had to run out and get it.

Mr. Purvis came over to us. "To save time,

I'm going to have you boys go next." He went back to the mike and announced us. I could hardly breathe. We all went up to the edge of the stage. I tried to see Mom in the audience, but the spotlight was so bright, I couldn't see anything. Brian adjusted his glasses and started reading our report. His voice droned on and on. Arful just sat there.

Dougie finally poked Brian in the ribs. "This is boring. Let's try the catnip." He had whispered right in front of the mike, so his voice boomed out over the audience. I could hear people laughing.

Then Brian lost his place and started reading the last part over again. Before we knew what was happening, Dougie ran over to Emily and came back with the bunch of catnip and the catnip mouse. He handed me the mouse. "Here, take this for a minute."

Then he got down on his hands and knees and held the catnip up to Arful's nose. "Come on, Arful," he whispered. "Take a whiff of this. You are a *caaaat*, remember? You love *caaaaatnip.*"

Arful blinked and sneezed.

I held the mouse up to my nose and took a big sniff. Whoa! What a great smell—even better than fish! I rubbed my face all over the mouse, then dropped it on the floor, and zinged it across the stage. Then I pounced on it and flipped it up in the air. I caught it in my teeth and chewed on it, letting out more of that great catnip smell. I could even taste it now.

What a fantastic toy! Why didn't they make toys for kids that smelled and tasted good? You could have action figures flavored with . . . maybe sardines! Would that be great, or what?

Brian and Dougie came running over and dragged me back to my seat. "Just sit here and stop clowning around," Brian said. "I thought you were supposed to be my friend." He looked as if he was going to cry. What did I do, anyway? I was just having some fun with a toy. Big deal.

Mr. Purvis was already at the mike, announcing Chad and Tony's obstacle course.

"But I'm not finished," Brian said.

Dougie put his hands on Brian's shoulders

and pushed him down into the chair next to me. "Yes, you are. We're all finished."

Chad and Tony started setting up. There were some hurdles, a big cloth tunnel held open by wire rings, and a couple of ramps.

Dougie sat on the other side of me. He still had the bunch of catnip. I grabbed it from him and buried my nose in the leaves. I wanted to laugh out loud. I wanted to throw the leaves on the floor and roll around in them. I wanted to crawl around on my hands and knees and rub my back against the legs of the chairs. I wanted to . . . . Suddenly Brian's foot kicked me in the leg. "Knock it off, Josh."

"Hmmmmmmm?"

Brian glared at me. "Haven't you done enough clowning around for one night?"

"What am I doing?"

Dougie was giving me a funny look. "You're purring."

"Of course I'm purring! I'm very happy! Do you mind?"

I slid off my chair and rolled across the stage. The obstacle course tunnel looked dark and mysterious—just the kind of place I loved

to explore. I had crawled halfway into it when I heard barking. Before I could turn around, I sniffed dog breath coming from the other end of the tunnel.

"Let *meeeowwwt* of here!" I yowled.

CHAPTER ELEVEN

What happened after that was kind of a blur. Tony's and Chad's dogs chased me across the stage, knocking over most of the hurdles. Then I hid under one of the ramps and watched everybody running around. The girls with the worms got scared and tried to run off the stage, but the one holding the tube tripped over a hurdle, spilling dirt and squirming worms everywhere.

That's when the parakeet came swooping down. I don't know if it wanted to eat the worms or just find a way out of there, but it zipped right past the spot where I was hiding. I lunged for it, and would have had it, if Mrs. Metz hadn't stepped into my path.

Then I was out in the open again, where the dogs could see me. I saw a light at the back of the auditorium where someone had just opened the door and I ran for it. Then I tore through the hall and slipped through the outside door as somebody was coming in.

As soon as I was outside, I headed for the big maple tree at the end of the playground and jumped up onto a branch in one leap. I clung to the bark, my heart pounding in my ears.

I could hear Mr. Purvis over the microphone, trying to get everyone to calm down. Then I heard him announce that Chad and Tony were going to try their obstacle course again. Good, that meant the dogs were still in the school. Strange dogs scared me.

Even though it was dark on the playground, I was surprised at how well I could see. There wasn't even a moon out, but I could see Dougie, Brian, and Arful coming across the playground plain as day.

"I know he came out here," Dougie said. "I saw him go out the door."

"I don't care if he is out here," Brian said. "I'm never speaking to him again. He messed up our project on purpose, just to be funny. I don't know why I was ever friends with him in the first place."

"I'm telling you, Brian, it's not like that. Josh couldn't help what he did. Look, there he is in the tree."

They ran over to me. "Get down here, Josh," Brian yelled.

"Why should I?"

"Because we need to help you," Dougie said.

"I don't need any help."

"You will after I get hold of you," Brian said. He turned to Dougie. "See? He's just playing games."

Dougie looked up. "Josh?"

"Yeah?"

"Do you think you're a cat?"

"What kind of a stupid question is that?" I said.

"Well, do you?"

"Of course. What else would I be?"

Dougie socked Brian in the arm. "I told you! Josh, you've got to get down here right away."

"Why?"

"Because we're going to hypnotize you back into being a kid."

"Why would I want to be a kid?"

"You *are* a kid," Dougie said. "You just think you're a cat, because the hypnosis worked on you instead of Arful. You don't even look like a cat."

I looked at my paws. "Yikes! I've got hands! I'm a cat with kid hands!"

"You've already made a fool of yourself," Brian said. "Don't make it any worse. Get down here."

I let go of the branch and landed on my back feet. Kid feet . . . in sneakers! I looked over my shoulder. "Hey! What happened to my tail?"

"This is terrible," Brian said. "We have to get him out of here."

Just then we heard some voices coming from the door to the school. "They must be out here somewhere, Mrs. Lewis. We'll find them."

"It's Mr. Purvis and Mom!" Brian whispered. "We're in big trouble now."

I heard a growl rise from my throat. "If

we're going into battle with Mr. Purvis, I need to sharpen my claws." I dug them into the rough bark of the tree and started scratching, but I soon found out that kid fingernails don't sharpen very well.

"We've got to get him switched back right now," Dougie said. "No telling what he'll do next."

"But I don't have the turban or the crystal," Brian whined.

"We don't have time for that. I'll do it. Just sit him down and hold him." Dougie fished around in his pocket. "I can use this."

Brian tackled me to the ground and Dougie started swinging a smiley face key chain in front of me. I was going to bat it away with my paw . . . hand . . . but then he started talking in this low soothing voice. "You are getting *sleeeepy*. Your eyelids are getting heavy." I could feel Arful's warm breath on my ear.

Blurry smiley face . . . two blurry smiley faces.

"You are a kid."

"Watch it," whispered Brian. "You don't

want to turn him into a goat. He's liable to butt old Mr. Purvis."

The smiley face came into focus and I could hear the voices getting closer. Then it started swinging again and got all blurry.

"Okay. You are NOT an animal . . . REPEAT . . . NOT any kind of animal. You are a human being. You are a boy."

Swing . . . swing . . . swing.

"You live in a house . . . you go to Percival Hatch Elementary School . . . You're in Mrs. Metz's third grade class."

Swing . . . swing . . . swing.

"You don't like to eat fish . . . you love pizza with pepperoni."

Back and forth . . . back and forth.

"When I snap my fingers, you will wake up and be a boy."

SNAP!

I woke up to find Dougie and Brian staring me in the face. "Well? Do you feel normal again?" Brian asked.

"I don't know. I just feel hungry is all."

"I want a pepperoni pizza."

"Me, too," Brian, Dougie, and I said at the same time.

Then we looked at one another. "Did you just say you wanted a pizza?" I asked.

"No, I did."

We all turned toward the voice and stared.

Arful smiled and licked his lips. "With anchovies," he added.

"Whoa!" Dougie said. "We're winning next year's science fair for sure!"

Don't Miss a Moment of the Funniest Family Feud Ever!

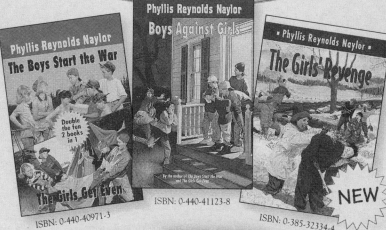

Phyllis Reynolds Naylor
The Boys Start the War
Double the fun 2 books in 1
The Girls Get Even
ISBN: 0-440-40971-3

Phyllis Reynolds Naylor
Boys Against Girls
By the author of *The Boys Start the War* and *The Girls Get Even*
ISBN: 0-440-41123-8

* Phyllis Reynolds Naylor *
The Girls' Revenge
ISBN: 0-385-32334-4

NEW